BATMAN

SCOOBY-DOO!

MYSTERIES

THE FRENZIED FELINE MYSTERY

by Michael Anthony Steele
illustrated by Dario Brizuela

Batman created by Bob Kane with Bill Finger

STONE ARCH BOOKS
a capstone imprint

Published by Stone Arch Books,
an imprint of Capstone.
1710 Roe Crest Drive
North Mankato, Minnesota 56003
capstonepub.com

Library of Congress Cataloging-in-Publication Data
Names: Steele, Michael Anthony, author. | Brizuela, Dario, illustrator.
Title: The frenzied feline mystery / by Michael Anthony Steele; illustrated
by Dario Brizuela.
Description: North Mankato, Minnesota : Stone Arch Books, [2022] | Series:
Batman and Scooby-Doo! mysteries | "Batman created by Bob Kane with Bill
Finger." | Audience: Ages 8–11. | Audience: Grades 4–6. | Summary: When a
wicked werecat plagues a big cat park on the outskirts of Gotham City, Mystery
Inc. joins forces with Batman to crack the case, but little do they know, more
than one crafty kitten is at play in the preserve.
Identifiers: LCCN 2021060107 (print) | LCCN 2021060108 (ebook) |
ISBN 9781666335194 (hardcover) | ISBN 9781666335217 (paperback) |
ISBN 9781666335224 (pdf)
Subjects: LCSH: Scooby-Doo (Fictitious character)—Juvenile fiction. | Batman
(Fictitious character)—Juvenile fiction. | Catwoman (Fictitious character)—
Juvenile fiction. | Superheroes—Juvenile fiction. | Animal sanctuaries—
Juvenile fiction. | Detective and mystery stories. | CYAC: Superheroes—Fiction.
| Animal sanctuaries—Fiction. | Adventure and adventurers—Fiction. | Mystery
and detective stories. | LCGFT: Detective and mystery fiction. | Superhero fiction.
Classification: LCC PZ7.S8147 Fp 2022 (print) | LCC PZ7.S8147 (ebook) | DDC
[Fic]—dc23
LC record available at https://lccn.loc.gov/2021060107
LC ebook record available at https://lccn.loc.gov/2021060108

Designer: Tracy Davies

Printed and bound in the USA. 4882

TABLE OF CONTENTS

CHAPTER 1

CAT ATTACK 6

CHAPTER 2

THE TRAP MISHAP 20

CHAPTER 3

LEAPING LEOPARDS 30

CHAPTER 4

TIGER TUSSLE 40

CHAPTER 5

A WILD RIDE 53

MEET BATMAN AND

BATMAN

While still a boy, Bruce Wayne watched his parents die at the hands of a petty criminal. After that tragic day, the young billionaire vowed to rid Gotham City of evil and keep its people safe. To achieve this goal, he trained his mind and body to become the World's Greatest Detective. Donning a costume inspired by a fearful run-in with bats at a young age, the Dark Knight now aims to strike the same sense of fear in his foes. But the Caped Crusader doesn't always work alone. He often teams up with other crime fighters, including Robin, Batgirl, Batwing, Batwoman, and even . . . Mystery Inc.

THE MYSTERY INC. GANG

Traveling in a van named the Mystery Machine, these meddling kids, and their crime-fighting canine, solve mysteries all over the country—even in Gotham City!

THE MYSTERY INC. GANG

Scooby-Doo

A happy hound with a super snout, Scooby-Doo is the mascot of Mystery Inc. He'll do anything for a Scooby Snack!

Shaggy Rogers

Shaggy is a laid-back dude who would rather search for food than clues . . . but he usually finds both!

Fred Jones, Jr.

Fred is the oldest member of the group. Friendly and fun-loving, he's a good sport—and good at them too.

Velma Dinkley

Velma is clever and book smart. She may be the youngest member of the team, but she's an old pro at cracking cases.

Daphne Blake

Brainy and bold, the fashion-forward Daphne solves mysteries with street smarts and a sense of style.

CHAPTER 1

CAT ATTACK

Daphne looked up from the map on her phone. "Turn left here," she instructed.

"You got it," Fred said as he spun the wheel.

The Mystery Machine turned down a narrow road. The sun was setting behind them and the Gotham City skyline loomed in the distance.

"This is so exciting," Velma said. "Mystery Inc. to the rescue once again."

Shaggy gulped. "Like, this isn't another haunted house is it?"

"Nope," Velma said, shaking her head.

Scooby-Doo wiped his brow. "Phew," he said.

"Then where are we going?" Shaggy asked.

"We've been asked to investigate the strange goings-on at an animal preserve," Fred replied.

Shaggy grinned. "Oh, like, that's not so bad."

"Reah," Scooby agreed.

"What kind of animals are we talking about?" Shaggy asked. "Like, exotic birds? Cute bunnies?"

"Guess again," Daphne said as she pointed to a sign up ahead.

The Mystery Machine drove past a billboard that read: *Gotham City Big Cat Preserve*. The sign showed photos of giant tigers, lions, and leopards.

"Rig cats?!" Scooby-Doo asked.

Shaggy gulped. "Like, Velma, I know you always say ghosts aren't real," he said. "But those big scary cats are very real."

"Don't worry, Shaggy," Velma said. "Preserves like this give safe homes to big cats who can't live in the wild anymore."

"Like, I just hope we're not showing up around feeding time," Shaggy said.

The Mystery Machine drove up to the main entrance. There were only three cars in the parking lot, so the gang got a spot right up front. Once they got out of the van, they spotted two men and a woman standing in front of the entrance.

"It's really a great deal," the woman told one of the men. "My company will pay top dollar."

"And the cats will be taken care of," added the shorter of the two men.

"I don't know . . . ," the third man said, shaking his head. Then he glanced up and smiled when he spotted the gang approaching. "I heard you were coming," he said, rushing up to shake Fred's hand. "I'm Parker Brooks, one of the owners of the preserve."

"Good to meet you, Mister Brooks," Fred said. "We're Mystery Inc."

"What seems to be the problem?" Velma asked.

"There's no problem," said the woman. "I'm Jeanette LeGalle, and my real-estate company is prepared to buy this property."

"And I'll buy all the cats," said the other man. "The name's Chris Howell, owner of the fabulous Howell Circus."

Mr. Brooks rubbed the back of his neck. "And the other owners and I just might have to sell," he said. "As long as there's a werecat around."

"Like, what's a werecat?" Shaggy asked.

"It's like a werewolf, but more of a scary cat monster," the man explained. "Long claws, sharp teeth. It's been scaring away our visitors."

"Zoinks!" Shaggy shouted as he leaped into Scooby-Doo's arms. "Big cats and a scary cat monster? Like, count me out!"

"Me too!" Scooby agreed.

"Come on, guys," Daphne said. "You don't believe in werecats, do you?"

Shaggy and Scooby glanced at each other and nodded their heads.

"Like, can't we just wait in the Mystery Machine this time?" Shaggy asked. "Please?"

"I guess that would be all right," Velma said. She leaned closer to the two friends. "After all, we already have two main suspects." She jutted a thumb at the people standing next to Mr. Brooks.

"Thanks!" Shaggy shouted as he and Scooby dashed toward the Mystery Machine. The van rocked as the door slammed behind them.

Mr. Brooks stepped over to a large vehicle covered with a metal cage. "That works out, since my cart only has six seats," he said as he opened a door on the cage.

"And I want to get a better look around," said Ms. LeGalle as she climbed aboard.

"Me too," agreed Mr. Howell.

Fred, Velma, and Daphne followed them onto the cart. Mr. Brooks climbed behind the wheel and closed the cage door. He drove them into the park.

"Is this cage here to protect us from the big cats?" Velma asked.

"Only if we drive into their enclosures," he replied. "Otherwise, all the cats are safely locked in their pens."

Mr. Brooks drove them past all the different cats' enclosures. They cruised past lions lounging on rocks, leopards climbing trees, and tigers splashing around a pool. A line of sky trolleys hung over the entire park so guests could view the cats from above.

Even though the sun had already set, large floodlights lit up everything. The cart moved along the main road with pens and storage buildings on each side.

"Look at all the cute kitties!" Daphne said.

"*Big* kitties," Fred added.

Ms. LeGalle pointed past the animals. "Think of all the houses we could build on this land."

"Think of all the tricks these cats could do in my circus," Mr. Howell added.

Velma shook her head. "Don't you think these cats would be happier here than in a circus?" she asked.

"Some of them came from a circus to begin with," Mr. Brooks said. "I think they're happier here but—"

SHOONK! Suddenly, the lights went out and the park went dark.

"Jeepers," Daphne said. "What happened?"

Mr. Brooks stopped the cart. "We're very close to the control center." He opened the cage and climbed out. "I'll go check on what happened." He marched toward the nearest building.

"See?" Ms. LeGalle said. "This place can't even keep the lights on. They have to sell."

"Maybe it's just a glitch," Velma suggested.

Yeeeeeaaaooooh!

A bloodcurdling scream came from the control center.

"What was that?" asked Mr. Howell. "Was it the werecat?"

"It sounded like Mister Brooks," Fred said as he got out of the cart. "Maybe he needs help!"

"I'm getting out of here while I still can," said Ms. LeGalle as she scrambled out of the cart.

"Me too!" agreed Mr. Howell as he ran after the woman. The two disappeared into the darkness.

Daphne and Velma followed Fred as he led the way to the control center. When Fred switched on his flashlight, they saw chairs toppled over and papers strewn everywhere.

Velma found a button on the nearby control console. She pushed it and the lights came back on. Several video screens came to life showing views from around the park.

"Where's Mister Brooks?" Daphne asked.

The man was nowhere to be found.

Pap, pap, pap, pap . . .

"What was that?" Fred asked.

"It sounds like someone is on the roof," Daphne replied.

The three ran outside and spotted a shadowy figure on top of the control center. The figure had pointed ears and a long tail. It moved with cat-like grace as it leaped from one building to the other.

"Jinkies," Velma said. "That looks like . . . a werecat!"

Shaggy and Scooby-Doo sat inside the back of the Mystery Machine. The two friends stacked bread, lunch meat, vegetables, and condiments to create two towering sandwiches.

"Like, this is the only way to solve mysteries, Scoob," Shaggy said.

"Rou said it!" Scooby-Doo agreed.

Just as the two friends prepared to down their giant sandwiches, the van's side door rattled.

"I guess Fred forgot his keys," Shaggy said. He turned to the side door of the van. "Like, the van is unlocked, come on in!"

The door flew open, but Fred wasn't on the other side. Shaggy and Scooby stared into the eyes of a growling monster! The cat-like beast was covered in striped gray fur and showed rows of sharp teeth as it snarled. It reached into the van with huge, clawed paws.

"Zoinks!" Shaggy yelled. "The werecat!"

Sandwich parts flew everywhere as Shaggy and Scooby scrambled for the back doors. As they tumbled out, the werecat climbed on top of the Mystery Machine and roared.

ROOOOOOOOOAR!

Shaggy and Scooby-Doo hugged each other as the werecat prepared to pounce.

Just then, something else roared.

VRRRRRRROOM!

It was a vehicle engine. Its bright headlights washed over them as it approached.

The werecat leaped off the van, but it didn't attack the two friends. Instead, it sailed over them and ran into the park entrance.

Shaggy and Scooby were still shivering as the long, black vehicle skidded to a stop beside them. The top hatch slid open, and a caped figure shot out of the car.

Shaggy's eyes widened.

"Batman!" he said.

CHAPTER 2

THE TRAP MISHAP

"Boy, am I glad to see you, Mister Batman, sir," Shaggy said.

Scooby nodded his head. "Reah!"

"What was that thing that ran into the park?" Batman asked.

Shaggy threw up his hands. "Like, only the biggest, scariest werecat you ever saw!"

Scooby-Doo growled and made a scary face. "Rith big teeth, and rarp claws . . ." He swiped the air with one paw.

Shaggy told the crime fighter what Mr. Brooks had said about the creature.

Batman's eyes narrowed. "Since werecats aren't real, there must be someone behind all this."

"Like, that's what Velma always says," Shaggy said. "But it looked pretty real to me."

Shaggy and Scooby led the Dark Knight through the park entrance. It wasn't long before they found the rest of the gang in the control center.

"Wow, it's Batman," Fred said.

"You bet," Shaggy agreed. "Like, Scoob and I wouldn't be in werecat territory without a Super Hero."

Shaggy and Scooby told the others about their run-in with the monster in the parking lot. Then Velma told Batman about Mr. Brooks's disappearance and their own werecat sighting.

"Zoinks!" Shaggy said. His teeth chattered. "T-t-two werecats?!"

"And *two* suspects," Velma added. She explained how Mr. Howell and Ms. LeGalle had run off. "Plenty of time for one of them to circle back and scare you in the parking lot."

As the teens explained what happened, Batman examined the wrecked control room. He picked up a tuft of gray fur and turned it over in his gloved hands.

Velma leaned closer for a better look.

"Gray fur?" she asked. "That doesn't look like it belongs to any big cat I've ever seen. I think it's a clue."

"I think you're right," the Caped Crusader said. He marched toward the exit. "It's time to find those missing people."

"And more clues," Daphne added.

The gang followed the crime fighter outside. As the Dark Knight led the way down the main pathway, Daphne and Velma followed close behind. Shaggy and Scooby brought up the rear.

"Like, I feel better solving this mystery with a Super Hero around," Shaggy said.

"Reah," Scooby agreed. "Me too!"

Fred grabbed Shaggy's shirt and Scooby-Doo's tail. "Not so fast, you two," he said. "While they search for clues, I need your help."

"Oh, boy," Shaggy said. "Like, let me guess. You want us to be bait for one of your traps."

Scooby nodded. "Rit must be rappin' time."

Fred grinned. "You know me so well."

With Shaggy and Scooby-Doo's help, Fred found a large metal cage with two openings. They dragged it to a dark part of the park and opened both sides.

"All you have to do is get one of the werecats to chase you into the cage," Fred explained. "You'll run through, and I'll close both doors to trap the creature inside."

Shaggy scratched his head. "Like, why don't Scoob and I close the doors and you run through?"

"Because I'm the trap expert," Fred replied. "And you two are experts at running from things."

Shaggy shrugged. "Well, he's got us there."

"Reah," Scooby agreed. "Rat's true."

Fred attached ropes to the doors and hid behind a nearby bush. Shaggy and Scooby walked down the main path in search of werecats.

"Like, h-h-here, k-k-kitty-kitty-kitty," Shaggy said as he trembled.

They saw plenty of big cats in their enclosures, but no werecats anywhere.

"Hey, Scoob," Shaggy said. "Like, maybe the werecats took the night off."

Just then, a low growl filled the night air.

GRRRRRRRR!

"I don't rink so, Raggy," Scooby-Doo replied. He raised a paw and pointed ahead of them. "Rook!"

A large cat stepped out of the shadows. It walked on four legs, so it wasn't the werecat. But its teeth looked just as sharp as a werecat's when it growled at them. It was a huge cougar.

"Like, I know you're not supposed to run from big cats in the wild," Shaggy said. His feet were already moving. "But I can't help it!"

"Me reither!" Scooby agreed as the two took off. They darted back the way they came from.

"I hope Fred is ready to trap a regular big cat," Shaggy said as they sprinted toward the open cage.

Shaggy was the first inside. His eyes went wide and he skidded to a stop.

WHAK!

Scooby-Doo slammed into his back. "What's wrong, Raggy?"

Shaggy pointed toward the other side of the open cage. "There's a-a-another c-c-cougar!"

A second cougar growled as it moved in from the other side. The two friends were trapped in the open cage as big cats crept toward them.

Just then, a shadowy figure landed atop the cage. The sleek creature was dressed in black and had short, pointed ears.

"Like, cougars on the ground and a werecat on top," Shaggy said. "We're doomed!"

Shaggy and Scooby-Doo hugged each other and closed their eyes.

The feline figure swiped at the ropes and the cage doors slammed shut.

BAM-BAM!

Shaggy opened one eye to see that they were safely locked inside the cage.

The werecat somersaulted off the cage and landed gracefully on the ground. Their unlikely rescuer gave a whistle, leading both cougars into a nearby enclosure. Once the cougars were safely locked up, the figure leaped to the roof of a nearby building and sprinted away.

"Wait a minute," Shaggy said, scratching his head. "Like, the werecat . . . saved us?"

CHAPTER 3

LEAPING LEOPARDS

Batman, Daphne, and Velma sprinted up just as Fred opened one of the cage doors. Shaggy explained how the werecat had saved them from the cougars.

Batman scanned the area. "Which way did it go?" he asked.

"Like, up there," Shaggy said as he pointed toward the nearby building.

The Dark Knight pulled his grapnel from his Utility Belt. He aimed it at the building and fired.

POP-WRRRR!

The grapnel latched onto the roof, and the device pulled Batman off the ground. His cape fluttered as he swung onto the roof and dashed out of sight.

Fred opened the other side of the cage. "Let's try again, guys," he said.

Daphne stiffened and her eyes went wide. "I think it's too late for that," she said.

"Aw, come on, Daphne," Fred said as he tied off one of the ropes. "It's never too late for a good trap."

Velma pointed toward the shadows. "It is when the monster shows up early. Look!"

GRRRRRRRR!

A snarling werecat stepped out of the shadows. It raised its razor-sharp claws as it charged toward the gang.

Everyone scattered as the vicious creature closed in. The beast locked in on Shaggy and Scooby-Doo and chased them through the park.

"Like, out of everyone, why does the werecat have to come after us?" Shaggy asked. "Haven't we already run enough for one mystery?"

"Rot really," Scooby replied.

Shaggy sighed. "I guess you're right."

The two friends pulled ahead and ducked inside a small storage shed. The werecat skidded to a stop and glanced around the building. It growled as it reached a clawed paw toward the door.

Just then, the door burst open and Shaggy and Scooby-Doo jumped out dressed as park rangers.

"Like, you're just in time for your grooming session," Shaggy said.

"Rat's right," Scooby-Doo agreed as he pulled a chair out of the shed and shoved it under the werecat.

The confused beast plopped into the chair just as Shaggy draped a cloth around its neck. Scooby pulled out a nail file and went to work on the claws on one of the beast's paws. Meanwhile, Shaggy began brushing out the creature's scruffy mane.

SWISH! SWISH! SWISH!

"Gotta look good for all the guests," Shaggy said as he brushed. "Like, when we're done with you, you'll be the star of the park!"

Scooby-Doo shoved a hand mirror into the beast's other paw. The werecat grinned as it admired its reflection. Meanwhile, Shaggy and Scooby reached down for an oversized bucket.

"Just one last thing," Shaggy said. "Like, it's time for your flea dip!"

The two friends dumped a bucket of water over the creature's head.

SPLOOSH!

They left the empty container on the monster's head as they both took off running again. The beast coughed and sputtered before throwing off the bucket.

ROOOOOOAR!

The werecat sprinted after them.

Shaggy and Scooby-Doo ditched the uniforms as they zigzagged through the park. The werecat rushed after them, determined to catch its prey.

Just as the monster closed in, Shaggy swung open a metal gate. Once he and Scooby-Doo ran through, he slammed it shut. **BAM!** The werecat smacked into the gate, snarling with rage.

Shaggy and Scooby held the gate shut, ready to keep the beast from getting through. Strangely, the werecat chuckled and disappeared into the night.

"Like, I don't get it, Scoob," Shaggy said. "Why did the werecat leave?"

Scooby-Doo whimpered as he tugged on Shaggy's shirt. "I know, Raggy."

Shaggy turned to see three huge leopards closing in. The big cats growled as they moved closer.

"Zoinks!" Shaggy shouted. "Like, we're in the leopard pen!"

Shaggy and Scooby took off as the large cats pounced. They ran around the pen with the leopards hot on their tails. The two friends cut across the area and scrambled up a tall tree in the center of the compound. The tree swayed as they reached the thinnest branches near the top.

"We should be safe up here, right, Scoob?" Shaggy asked.

Scooby-Doo clung to a thin branch and glanced down. "Ruh-Roh," he said.

Below them, the three leopards began to climb. Their sharp claws dug into the bark as they made their way toward the two friends.

"Like, I really don't want to be cat food," Shaggy said.

Just then, a big, red ball sailed over the fence. It bounced into the center of the enclosure. The leopard closest to Shaggy and Scooby hopped down and ran up to the ball. The big cat batted it around with one paw before jumping up to balance on top. After a couple of shaky steps, the leopard walked atop the ball, rolling it around the pen.

"Well, would you look at that, Scoob," Shaggy said.

"Rat's weird," Scooby-Doo replied.

Two more balls flew into the pen, and the other leopards were on them in a flash. Soon, all three cats rolled around like circus performers.

"Like, let's get out of here while we can," Shaggy suggested.

Just as the two friends were about to climb down, Batman swung toward them. He snatched them out of the tree and sailed over the fence.

"Thanks for the save, Mister Batman, sir," Shaggy said as the three lightly touched down.

"Reah," Scooby agreed.

"And, like, throwing in those balls was the perfect distraction," Shaggy added.

"Those weren't my idea," said the Dark Knight.

"Then who threw them?" Shaggy asked.

Batman's eyes narrowed. "I don't know."

CHAPTER 4

TIGER TUSSLE

"So, you think one of the werecats saved you again?" Daphne asked.

Shaggy rubbed the back of his neck. "Yeah, like, I guess so."

"Mister Brooks did say some of the cats came from a circus," Velma added. "That must be why the leopards knew how to balance on those balls."

"It looks as if we have *two* mysteries on our hands," Fred said. "Who are the werecats? And why is one of them so helpful?"

Velma pointed toward the cable cars moving over the park. "I bet we can spot both werecats from up there."

"Good idea," Batman said.

"Uh-uh, no thanks," Shaggy said, shaking his head. "Like, I'm staying on solid ground from now on."

"Reah," Scooby-Doo said, nodding his head. "What he said."

Batman pulled a small radio from his Utility Belt. "Here," he said, handing it to Velma. "Let me know if you spot anything."

"Yes, sir," Velma said before she, Daphne, and Fred took off toward the nearby cable car loading platform.

The three friends climbed aboard one of the open cars and shut the door behind them. Fred reached out and pulled the lever. The car rocked forward as the cable pulled it high above the grounds. They slowly moved between the many suspension towers spaced throughout the park.

Daphne aimed a pair of binoculars at the park below them. "We should be able to see the werecat from up here," she said. "In fact, I have a great view of all the cats."

"Hold the phone," Fred said. "I just spotted the werecat!"

Velma leaned over the car's railing, scanning the grounds. "Where?" she asked. "I don't see anything."

Fred tapped her shoulder and pointed to one of the approaching towers. "There!" he said. The werecat climbed up the tall structure to meet them. "And we're heading right for it!"

"Jinkies!" Velma cried. She reached out and aimed Daphne's binoculars at the approaching tower.

Daphne flinched when she spotted the creature. "Jeepers!" she said, lowering the binoculars. She glanced around the car. "How can we stop this thing?"

Fred shrugged. "I don't think we can."

Velma pressed a button on the radio. "Batman, we found the werecat," she reported. "Actually, it found us!"

Back on the ground, Batman's head snapped up toward the cable car. He spotted the gang's car immediately. His lips tightened when he saw it approaching the creature climbing the tower.

"Like, the werecat is going to get them!" Shaggy shouted. "What do we do?"

"Get to the control center," Batman replied. "Find a button that stops the cable cars."

"Yes, sir!" Scooby-Doo replied with a salute. He and Shaggy ran toward the control center.

The Dark Knight pulled out his grapnel and aimed it up at the car.

POP-WRRRR!

The crime fighter's cape flapped behind him as he zipped up to the cable car. He swung inside just as the werecat leaped from the tower. The beast snarled as it landed inside the car.

The kids scrambled clear as Batman went on the attack. He grabbed the roof of the car and swung toward the beast.

SMAK! His boots slammed into the creature, knocking it against the back of the car. With lightning speed, the beast leaped to its feet and slashed at Batman with its sharp claws, driving the hero back.

"We're running out of room," Fred said as the three of them moved behind the Dark Knight.

GRRRRRRR!

The werecat growled as it charged toward the hero. Batman caught its claws in both hands, but the creature drove the Super Hero back and slammed him into the kids.

AAAAAAAAAH!

Fred, Daphne, and Velma screamed as they tumbled out of the car. Luckily, Fred latched onto the railing with both hands. Velma grabbed onto his legs, and Daphne held onto Velma's. They dangled high above the park.

Shaggy and Scooby-Doo raced into the control room. Shaggy's heart dropped when he spotted one of the video screens. It showed his friends dangling from the cable car.

"Zoinks!" Shaggy shouted. "Like, the gang is about to fall to their doom!"

Scooby-Doo scanned the many buttons and levers on the panel. "Rhere's the stop button?" He raised a paw over a big red button, ready to push it.

"Hold it, Scoob!" Shaggy shouted. He pointed to a label right above the button. It read *Open All Cages.* "Like, you nearly had us crawling with cats!"

Scooby-Doo wiped his brow. "Whew!"

Shaggy scanned the panel and found the emergency stop button for the cable cars. But before he pushed it, he checked the video screen again. "Like, check it out, buddy," he said, pointing to the screen. "If I wait a few seconds, I can stop the car over that big swimming pool," he said. "Then they can just drop into the water."

"Rood idea, Raggy," Scooby said.

Shaggy held his hand over the button. When the car was above the pool, he slammed the button. The cable car stopped.

Shaggy grinned and dusted off his hands.

Scooby-Doo's eyes widened. "Rad idea, Raggy," he said, pointing at the screen.

Several tigers dove into the swimming pool, waiting for their dangling friends to drop.

"Worse than that," Shaggy said, pointing to another screen. "There's the other werecat."

Another screen showed a viewing room below the pool's surface where guests could watch the tigers swim. A sleek, feline figure watched the action from behind the thick glass.

"Like, I can't believe I'm saying this," Shaggy said with a gulp. "But we have to go help—even though the second werecat is already there."

"Are you sure?" Scooby-Doo asked with a shiver.

Shaggy gave a nervous chuckle. "Not really. But, like, our friends need us, Scoob."

The pair dashed out of the control room just as their friends fell into the pool.

Batman's cape swirled as he performed a spinning kick, knocking the beast back to the other side of the car. The creature breathed heavily as it staggered to its feet. The crime fighter knew he could easily defeat the beast, but he had something else to worry about. He glanced out of the car to see the three kids treading water in the pool below. Three tigers surrounded them, swimming closer and closer.

The Dark Knight dove from the cable car.

WHOOSH!

The crime fighter splashed into the pool and swam between the gang and the nearest tiger. With all his might, he grabbed the big cat and flung it to the far end of the pool. Two more tigers came at them from the other side. Batman wasn't sure how to keep all the cats away from the swimming kids.

Shaggy and Scooby-Doo raced into the viewing room. They skidded to a stop when they found themselves face-to-face with the second werecat.

Shaggy shook his head. "Wait a minute," he said. "Like, you're no werecat!"

Although the woman standing there wore a black bodysuit and had cat-like ears, she wasn't a monster at all.

Shaggy pointed at her. "Like, you're Gotham City's famous cat burglar, Catwoman!"

"Good eye," Catwoman said. She strolled to the wall of thick glass. "And it looks as if I have to save the day again." She pulled out a tool with a sparkling diamond tip. She expertly cut a large circle in the glass, just below the waterline.

POP-WHOOOOSH!

A large circle of glass popped out, and water from the pool poured through the hole. Along with the water, Fred, Daphne, and Velma tumbled out. They coughed and sputtered as they stumbled to their feet. After Batman washed through, he grabbed an object from his Utility Belt and flung it toward the glass.

WHHHP!

The small net expanded and stuck to the glass. It covered the hole, keeping the tigers from following.

CHAPTER 5

A WILD RIDE

"What are you doing here, Catwoman?" Batman asked. "There are no priceless diamonds to steal."

"There's more to me than cat burglary," the criminal replied. She moved to a nearby closet and pulled out several fluffy towels. She handed them out to the group. "I volunteer here sometimes because I don't want these big cats to lose their home. I want to find out who's behind this werecat as much as you do."

After the group moved outside, Fred pointed up to the cable car dangling above the tiger pool. "The werecat's gone," he said.

"But I see another cat," Daphne said.

"Rhere? Rhere?" Scooby-Doo asked as he leaped into Shaggy's arms. The two friends' eyes went wide as they scanned the area.

Daphne pointed to the ground. "Right here," she said. A small cat strolled up to Daphne and rubbed against her legs. She picked it up and cradled it in her arms. The cute kitty began to purr as she scratched it behind the ears. "How did a house cat like you end up in a place like this?" she asked.

"Uh, that's not a house cat," Catwoman said. "That's a lion cub."

"Oh, boy," Velma said. "And where there's a baby lion, the mother isn't far behind."

GRRRRRR!

The cub's mother growled as she ambled out of the shadows. Daphne placed the cub on the ground and backed toward the rest of the group.

"How did she get out of her pen?" Fred asked.

Shaggy dropped Scooby-Doo and then leaped into his arms. He pointed in another direction. "Like, she isn't alone. Look!"

More big cats slowly closed in. The group was surrounded by tigers, leopards, lions, and cougars. The animals growled as they circled.

"Someone must've opened all the cages," Velma said.

"Like, I saw a button that did that in the control room," Shaggy said.

"Reah," Scooby-Doo agreed.

"There's a button next to it that rings the dinner bell," Catwoman reported. "If you push it, all the cats should return to their enclosures."

Batman pulled a set of bolas from his Utility Belt. With a flick of his wrist, he spun the balls at the end of their ropes.

WHP-WHP-WHP-WHP . . .

Catwoman uncoiled a long whip from around her waist. Standing back-to-back with Batman, she cracked the whip.

WHP-KRAK!

The big cats snarled but kept their distance. Some even backed away.

"We'll hold them off while you get to the control room," Batman said.

Shaggy's eyes darted back and forth at the surrounding cats. "Like, how are we going to do that?"

Fred grinned. "That's how," he said, pointing to the nearby caged cart. "Come on, gang. It's time to roll!"

With Batman and Catwoman keeping the big cats back, the group moved toward the cart. Mystery Inc. piled in and closed the cage behind them. They sped off, leaving the crime fighter and the cat burglar to occupy the cats.

Unfortunately, a lion and a tiger took off after the cart. They caught up and leaped onto the cage.

"Like, no hitchhikers," Shaggy said.

"Reah," Scooby said. "Bad kitties!"

Fred jerked the wheel back and forth, but he couldn't shake the cats from the top of the cart.

"Someone's going to have to jump for it," Fred said.

"Like, I'll take the wheel while you do that," Shaggy suggested.

Velma shook her head. "It has to be you and Scooby," she said.

"She's right," Daphne agreed. "You know where the button is."

The two friends glanced at each other before shaking their heads.

"Ruh-uh," Scooby said.

"No way," Shaggy added.

Velma reached into her pocket. "Would you each do it for a Scooby Snack?" She pulled out two small treats.

Shaggy crossed his arms. "Like, we can't be bribed by a little . . ."

Velma pulled out two more treats. "*Two* Scooby Snacks?"

"Done!" Shaggy agreed.

Velma tossed the treats, and the two friends downed them in one gulp.

"Get ready," Fred warned as they neared the control center.

When the cart was close to the building, Shaggy and Scooby bailed out. They ran through the door and slammed it behind them in case any of the cats chased them.

Unfortunately, they had locked themselves inside with . . .

"The werecat!" Shaggy shouted.

The tall beast stood in the center of the room. It snarled with a mouthful of sharp teeth.

Shaggy glanced at the button on the control panel. "Like, can you distract him, Scoob?"

Just then, the monster lunged. Shaggy ran for the controls while Scooby-Doo circled the room with the werecat hot on his tail.

"I'm ristracting him!" Scooby shouted. "I'm ristracting him!"

Shaggy slammed a hand onto the button.

DING-DING-DING-DING!

A loud bell sounded from outside.

"Like, let's get out of here," Shaggy said as he threw open the door.

He and Scooby-Doo scrambled outside with the werecat close behind. They leaped onto the caged cart just as Fred drove by. The lion and the tiger were no longer there. The dinner bell must've worked. Unfortunately, the werecat jumped onto the cart with them.

"Help!" Shaggy said. "Like, I guess this werecat didn't hear the bell!"

"I have an idea," Fred said. "But you're not going to like it."

"Wait, what?" Shaggy asked.

"Get ready to jump," Fred ordered as he turned the cart toward some construction equipment in front of a tall fence. Fred drove the cart up the back of a trailer that was pointed up like a ramp.

"Jump!" Fred ordered. He, Daphne, and Velma leaped out of the cage.

VROOOM!

Shaggy jumped from the top, just as the cart flew off the back of the ramp. Scooby-Doo was about to join him, but the werecat grabbed his tail at the last minute.

"Scoob!" Shaggy shouted as he got to his feet.

WHOOSH!

Just then, Batman swooped in and snatched the dog from the top of the cart. As he carried Scooby-Doo to safety, the cart landed in the middle of the lion pen.

KRASH!

Everyone ran to the railing to see the werecat standing atop the cart while several lions surrounded him.

"Help!" the werecat shouted. "Help!"

Catwoman smirked. "Werecats can't talk, can they?"

SLAM!

A door swung open from a nearby building. Ms. LeGalle and Mr. Howell bolted out. They ran up to the others.

"We heard the bell," Ms. LeGalle said. "Is it safe to come out?"

"It is now," Velma said. "And since you two are here, it's also safe to say that this mystery is finally solved."

POP-WRRRR!

Batman fired his grapnel and swung out into the lion pen. He scooped up the werecat and looped back to the others. Once they were safely on the ground, the Dark Knight pulled off the werecat's mask.

"Mister Brooks?" Fred asked.

The man shook his head. "I wanted to scare everyone away so I could convince the other owners to sell." He frowned as he looked at everyone. "And I would've gotten away with it if it weren't for you meddling kids."

"And Batman," Shaggy said.

"And Catwoman," Daphne added. She glanced around. "Wait, where'd she go?" The cat burglar was gone.

Scooby-Doo giggled. "Rooby-dooby doo!"

CATWOMAN

Real Name: Selina Kyle

Occupation: Professional Thief

Base: Gotham City

Height: 5 feet 7 inches

Weight: 125 pounds

Eyes: Green

Hair: Black

Powers/Abilities:
Top-notch agility, reflexes, and acrobatic skills, master of thievery

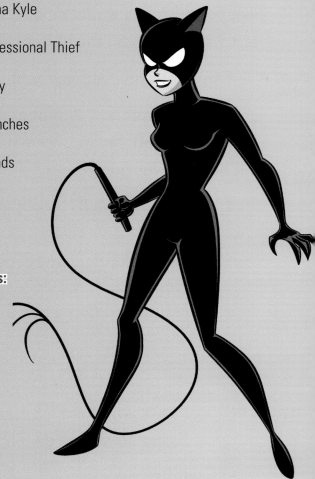

Biography: Like Bruce Wayne, Selina Kyle was orphaned at a young age. But unlike Bruce, Selina had no caretakers or family fortune to support her. Growing up alone on the mean streets of Gotham City, Selina was forced to resort to petty crime in order to survive. She soon became one of the city's most dangerous criminals. Becoming Catwoman to hide her true identity, Selina prowls the streets of Gotham City, preying on the wealthy while guarding Gotham City's fellow castaways.

- Selina's love of felines led her to choose a cat-related nickname. In fact, much of her stolen loot has been donated to cat-saving charities throughout the world.

- The athletic Selina prefers to use her feline grace and cat-like agility to evade her would-be captors. But when push comes to shove, Catwoman can use her retractable claws to keep her opponents at a distance.

- Selina has been an ally to Batman on several occasions. When a deadly plague spread through Gotham City, Catwoman teamed up with the Caped Crusader to help find a cure. However, their alliances never last, since Selina seems uninterested in putting an end to her thieving ways.

BIOGRAPHIES

photo by M. A. Steele

Michael Anthony Steele has been in the entertainment industry for more than 28 years, writing for television, movies, and video games. He has authored more than 120 books for exciting characters and brands including Batman, Superman, Wonder Woman, Spider-Man, Shrek, Scooby-Doo, WISHBONE, LEGO City, Garfield, Night at the Museum, and The Penguins of Madagascar. Steele lives on a ranch in Texas, but he enjoys meeting his readers when he visits schools and libraries all across the country. For more information, visit MichaelAnthonySteele.com.

photo by Dario Brizuela

Dario Brizuela works traditionally and digitally in many different illustration styles. His work can be found in a wide range of properties, including Star Wars Tales, DC Super Hero Girls, DC Super Friends, Transformers, Scooby-Doo! Team-Up, and more. Brizuela lives in Buenos Aires, Argentina.

GLOSSARY

cable car (KAY-buhl KAR)—a vehicle pulled along by a moving cable, often used for carrying people above parks or up mountains

console (KON-sole)—a cabinet with the controls for electronic equipment

enclosure (en-KLOH-zhur)—an area closed in by a fence or walls

feline (FEE-line)—having to do with cats; any animal of the cat family

grapnel (GRAP-nuhl)—a grappling hook connected to a rope that can be fired like a gun

preserve (pri-ZURV)—a place where animals can live and be protected from hunters

real-estate (REEL-eh-state)—land and the buildings on it that can be bought or sold

suspect (SUHSS-pekt)—someone thought to be responsible for a crime

suspension tower (suh-SPEN-shuhn TOU-ur)—a tall pole that holds up wires or cables

territory (TER-uh-tor-ee)—an area of land that an animal claims as its own to live in

vicious (VISH-uhss)—fierce or dangerous

THINK ABOUT IT

1. At the start of the story, Velma thinks Ms. LeGalle and Mr. Howell are the main suspects behind the mystery of the werecat. Why do you think she suspected them and not Mr. Brooks?

2. Catwoman helps Batman and the Mystery Inc. gang in this story. Do you think that makes her a hero, or is she still a villain? Explain your answer.

3. Mr. Brooks dresses up as a werecat to scare away visitors to the big cat preserve. Why do you think he pretended to be that kind of monster?

WRITE ABOUT IT

1. Fred loves to build traps to catch monsters. Imagine that you could build a trap to safely catch a werecat. Write a paragraph describing your trap, then draw a picture of it.

2. Catwoman says she sometimes volunteers at the big cat preserve. Write about a time you volunteered somewhere and explain why you did it.

3. At the end of the story, Catwoman suddenly disappears. What happens next? Write a new chapter describing where she goes and what she does on her next adventure. You decide!

READ THEM ALL!